Millie Muldoon & the Christmas Mystery

By

Mary Vigliante Szydlowski

Text Copyright © 2016

Mary Vigliante Szydlowski

All rights reserved. This book or any portion thereof may not be reproduced or used in any manner whatsoever without the express written permission of the publisher except for the use of brief quotations in a book review.

To Nate,

Merry 1st Christmas little guy! You're the best present your Grandma and Grandpa could have ever wished for. You've brought happiness and good cheer to our lives! Every day is Christmas now!

Table of Contents

Chapter 1..7

Chapter 2..9

Chapter 3..13

Chapter 4..15

Chapter 5..18

Chapter 6..26

Chapter 7..32

Chapter 8..36

Chapter 9..41

A Note From Mary Vigliante Szydlowski.....43

About the Author................................44

Chapter 1

Someone was crying. They were sniffling and boohooing loud enough to wake the dead.

Half asleep, Millie Muldoon stuck her nose out from under the blanket. She looked around, but couldn't see a thing. The room was pitch black. She looked at the clock on her nightstand, trying to focus on the glowing green numbers. It was nearly midnight.

"Be quiet," she threatened. It was hard to tell who was making all the racket. "Go to sleep!" she hissed.

The house was overflowing with relatives visiting for the Christmas holiday. Millie's Grandma and Grandpa Langella and her Great Aunt Priscilla Palermo were sleeping in the two spare bedrooms. Three sets of aunts and uncles were camped out in the den, the attic loft, and the basement playroom.

Since her bedroom was bigger than her little brother Roger's, she got stuck with her seven boy cousins. They were sleeping side by side on the floor. Packed in together like sardines in a can.

She suspected that it was Brian, one of the Larabee cousins, who was making all the noise. He was always crying about something or other.

There were more sniffles and whimpers. Another kid was crying. This one was so loud he woke up Millie's pet hamster

Snuggles. She could hear Snuggles digging around in her cage.

Millie groaned. She knew what was coming next. The chubby, little furball hopped on her exercise wheel. A second later the room was filled with squeaks and creaks as the wheel began to turn. The faster it went the louder it got.

"Oh no! Now see what you've done!" Click! Rattle! **Squeal!** Click! Rattle! **Screech!** "No Snuggles! It's nighty-night time! Not playtime! And as for the rest of you…**be quiet!"** she ordered. "It's Christmas Eve! You're supposed to be asleep! If Santa comes to the house and hears you carrying on like this, he won't come down the chimney. And if he doesn't come down the chimney, he won't leave us any presents. No Santa! No presents! Understand!"

The sobs grew louder and louder. More children began to cry.

Millie sat up in bed. She was past the point of being annoyed. She was mad! It was bad enough that they'd taken over her room. That they'd messed with her toys. That they'd kept her awake with their squirming and snoring. But this…this was too much! They were going to ruin Christmas if they kept this up!

She'd been extra good all year. She'd made her bed every day. She'd kept her room clean. She'd helped out with the dishes and around the house. She'd studied hard in school. Why she'd even been polite to old Mrs. Chambers. The nasty neighbor lady who gave dirty looks to everyone who walked by her house.

Millie was sure Santa would reward her hard work and good behavior. With the one thing she wanted most in the world...a purple, ten-speed bicycle.

She was not about to let these crybabies wreck Christmas for her!

Millie didn't like little boys very much to begin with. All they did was make messes and cause problems. Right now they were keeping her awake and that was making her very cranky! If it weren't for this bunch of whiners, she'd be fast asleep right now. Hugging her teddy bear, Clarence, and dreaming sweet dreams of zooming down Maple St. hill on her shiny new bike.

"I'm warning you," she threatened. "If you don't stop this right now, Santa won't come."

She'd expected them to quiet them down at once, but they didn't. They cried even harder! The more they cried, the angrier she got. **She'd had enough of their foolishness!** Millie reached over and turned on her bedside lamp.

The room went silent. The boys trembled in terror when they saw her. They were afraid to even breathe. Boy did she look mad! Her face was red with rage. Her blue eyes glaring at them. Her brown braids looking like wild, wiggling snakes.

Millie looked around the room. The blond Konitski brothers, Chris and Richard, were sobbing in the corner. The dark-haired Rossi boys: David, Peter, and Vincent, were sniffling, their eyes brimming with tears. Next to them were the redheaded Larabees: Tom and Brian, who were definitely the worst of the bunch. They were bawling like someone in their family had died. Like they'd lost their best friend. **Very dramatic! Hugely annoying!**

She looked up and saw her little brother Roger standing in the doorway. Her eyes narrowed. He wasn't allowed to set foot in her room without her permission. And she hadn't given him permission! She glared at him.

It was bad enough having boy cousins, but having a messy little brother was even worse! The others only visited every once in a while, but Roger was underfoot all the time. He was always sneaking around. Trying to play with her toys and touch her books. Getting sticky fingerprints on her furniture and walls. Sneezing and coughing and spreading his germs all over her room.

She'd been happy being an only child. Everything had been neat and tidy then. The house quiet and peaceful. But then *he* came along…with his dirty little hands and bad habits! He burped and farted and picked his nose. His fingernails were gross. And he never remembered to flush. Yuck! **Why couldn't her parents have left well enough alone!**

Seeing the nasty look on his sister's face, Roger quickly

stepped back into the hall. Millie wasn't very nice when she was in a good mood. She was always cranky and crabby! But, when she was in a bad mood.... she was absolutely awful! Roger thought it best to stay out of her way.

Sad and scared, he swallowed hard. Then, using a trembling fist, he rubbed away his tears. He didn't want Millie calling him a crybaby. Like she sometimes did when she was being mean.

"What's going on?" she demanded to know.

The Konitskis looked at the Larabees. The Rossis looked at the Konitskis. But nobody said a word. Finally, they all turned to Roger.

"She's your sister," Brian whispered. "You tell her!"

Roger looked horrified. ***Why him?*** She wasn't going to like this. She wasn't going to like this at all!

He started to open his mouth, but the words caught in his throat. Even though he tried hard not to, tears filled his eyeS. He started to cry again.

Millie drummed her fingers on the mattress. She was waiting for an explanation. Irritated, she got up on her knees and looked at her brother. She gave Roger her dirtiest, scariest scowl. "I want to know what's going on," she growled. "And I want to know ***right now!***" With that she threw her feet over the side of the bed. Before he could respond, she charged toward him.

"Santa's already been here!" he blurted out. That stopped her dead in her tracks. "We heard noises outside. We peeked out the window and saw footprints in the snow. We weren't sure it was Santa at first, but then his reindeer started walking around on the roof. So we figured it must be. We heard voices coming from the back of the house. We thought Santa might be talking to one of his elves so we opened the window a crack to listen. That's when we heard him jiggling the knob on the back door and fiddling with the kitchen windows and the patio door. We figured he must have gained a lot of weight this year and was too fat to get down our chimney. He was trying to find another way into the house. We waited until the noise stopped and everything was quite again. Then we sneaked downstairs to see the presents."

Millie clapped her hands and began dancing around the room on her tippy-toes. The grin on her face stretched from ear to ear. She couldn't wait to see her new bike. She was heading toward the door when she suddenly stopped. Why was she the only one happy about Santa's visit? Why was she the only one going downstairs to look under the tree? ***Something was wrong. Very wrong!*** Instead of smiles and laughter, she was surrounded by a roomful of sad, gloomy faces, runny noses, and tears. This was not the way children were supposed to look or behave. Not on Christmas Eve! Not when they'd just been visited by Santa Claus!

"What's the matter?" Millie asked in a nervous whisper,

starting to get concerned. She knew something bad must have happened. Maybe they hadn't gotten all the gifts they'd asked for this year.

"Santa didn't leave any presents this year!" Roger told her. Tears streaming down his chubby cheeks.

"What!" She was stunned! Perhaps he meant that Santa had forgotten to leave their cousins' presents under the tree. Maybe he'd dropped the presents off at their own houses instead. "Do you mean that there aren't ***many*** presents under the tree?" she asked. "Or that there aren't ***any***?"

"There aren't any," he whimpered. "There's nothing under the tree. Not a single present!"

"You can't be serious!" She couldn't believe it!. This was worse than she'd imagined. This was awful! No, this was worse than awful! This was terrible! It was an absolute disaster! A nightmare! This couldn't be happening!

Roger nodded that he was.

"There must be some mistake! It's not that late! It's only midnight. Santa works all night long on Christmas Eve. Into the wee hours of the morning. It's not even the middle of the night yet. It's still early. He probably hasn't even been here yet," she countered. She was trying to come up with a good reason why they'd found nothing under the tree. "Maybe the noises you heard had nothing to do with Santa. They could have been caused by icicles falling off the roof, gusts of wind, branches tapping at the windows, or the neighbors taking out the garbage!"

"No! He's been here all right," Chris Konitski told her. "He must have come down the chimney. The fireplace screen is knocked over. He drank all the milk we put out for him. And ate every cookie on the plate. But…but…" he said sobbing uncontrollably, "he didn't fill our stockings or leave us any presents."

Millie staggered backward and collapsed on the bed. This was dreadful! The worst thing that had ever happened to her in her whole entire life!

Chapter 2

Millie looked around at the unhappy faces. The boys were all little monsters. They were messy, and sloppy, and always getting into trouble. But they didn't deserve this! She thought Santa would be more understanding. He was a little boy once wasn't he? Sure they made mistakes and got into mischief sometimes, but they tried hard to be good. Didn't that count for anything? It didn't seem fair that Santa would suddenly get strict without warning people first.

Millie brought her hand to her head and began scratching.

"What's she doing?" Chris asked his older brother Richard. He was nine and very wise. "Does she have an itch or something?"

"Shhh. No. She's thinking," he whispered, bringing a finger to his lips. He wanted everyone to be quiet. Millie was a good detective. Maybe she could figure out what was going on and why there weren't any presents under the tree this year.

Millie didn't say a word. She thought and thought, then thought some more. Millie was smart. She always knew all the answers. Always knew what to do. But not this time. This time she didn't have a clue. She searched her brain for a solution to the mystery of the missing presents. What in the world could have happened to make Santa behave like this? Was he mad at them? And if so…*why?*

Millie tried to come up with reasons for Santa's strange

behavior. Maybe he wasn't angry. Maybe he just forgot to put the presents out this year.

Could he have gotten so involved in eating the cookies or drinking the milk that the gifts slipped his mind? Was that possible? The old gent was getting on in years. Maybe he was getting a little forgetful.

She thought about it a while, then shook her head. No, that couldn't be it. Santa might be old, but he was the smartest man alive. That's how he knew which children were naughty and which ones were nice. And who wanted what toys for Christmas. A jolly old elf like Santa wouldn't have memory lapses! But if that wasn't the answer, what was?

"Hmmm," she said to no one in particular. She was thoughtfully tapping her chin with a finger. There was a lot of cold and flu going around this year. Could Santa have suddenly felt ill? Gone outside for some fresh air? That would explain the footprints in the snow. Or worse still, perhaps Santa was so sick that he had to stay home this year. Maybe one of his bumbling, absent-minded elves was delivering the presents for him. Again she shook her head. That couldn't be it either. Santa was magic. She didn't think he ever got sick! Especially not on Christmas Eve! The most important night of the year!

She started to fiddle with her hair. Could he have been called away on an emergency? Maybe a reindeer got hurt? Or maybe something happened to Mrs. Claus? Or one of his elves back at the North Pole? Anything was possible, of course, but she didn't think so. Reindeer graceful enough to fly through the air wouldn't be clumsy enough to fall off a roof or trip on the ice. And if there was a problem at the North Pole? Well surely one of his elves could take care of it until Santa was done with his deliveries.

Millie was running out of ideas.

She began twisting her braids. Perhaps Santa left something at the last house he'd stopped at. And then had to go back for it. That sounded reasonable! More reasonable than anything she'd come up with so far. But why hadn't he come back with their presents? There had to be a reason. She just didn't know what it was yet!

Suppose he had to call the North Pole for some reason. And he'd forgotten to bring his cell phone. Or his battery was low. Or he couldn't get a signal. Could he have gone out to find a payphone and then got lost trying to find his way back? The only place she knew that still had one was the Quick Stop. It was down the road, only a mile away. The more she thought about it, the dumber it sounded. Santa could have used the landline phone in the living room. It was on the same table with the cookies and milk. Mom and Dad wouldn't have minded. Even if it was long distance! He'd been coming to her house since she was a baby. It didn't seem likely that he'd lose his way after all these years.

Could Santa have put his naughty and nice list on his laptop computer? Could there have been a power failure at the North Pole or some kind of glitch in the software? Could his system have crashed? Deleting the master list of good little boys and girls and the gifts they wanted for Christmas? Or maybe trolls hacked into his system and switched their names from the nice to the naughty list?

Very unlikely! Besides, that explanation didn't fit the facts in the case. Santa had been here. He'd eaten the cookies and drank the milk. He couldn't have mistaken her house for a diner! He'd been here for a reason: to bring the children their presents. But then why hadn't he?

Her head hurt from all the thinking, but she was no closer to an answer. To solve the mystery, Millie would have to play detective. She'd have to investigate the case. Search for clues. Then figure out what happened.

Millie went to her desk and opened the drawer. She pulled out her magnifying glass. **She'd get to the bottom of this, if it was the last thing she did!**

Chapter 3

Roger was leaning against the doorway. He was crying. Millie couldn't help but feel sorry for him. He looked heartbroken. She walked up to her little brother. Then, holding her breath, as though she was about to touch something yucky...like a spider or a worm, she patted his head. It wasn't that she liked him any better. But Millie was his big sister. Whether she liked it or not, she had to be nice to him every once in a while.

His body shook with sobs. He was thinking about the red tricycle he wanted for Christmas. He looked so sad. Millie almost felt bad for all the times she'd been mean to him. Telling him there were monsters living under his bed. And gremlins and ogres hiding in his closet waiting to grab him and plop him in a stew.

She supposed that as little brothers went, she probably shouldn't complain. She could have done much worse. She could have gotten Sophie Kirsch's baby brother. He was like a puppy. He left puddles all over the house. Or Tia Carey's. He liked to wash his hands in her aquarium. Or, even worse, Libby Owens' little brother. He grossed people out by snorting and shooting buggers out his nose and burping the alphabet. And he liked to follow people around and fart. Compared to that, Roger didn't seem all that bad. She was thankful that the worst thing the little pest did was forget to put the toilet seat down. Or leave a dirty ring around the bathtub.

She stared down at her hand, wondering how many of

Roger's germs had rubbed off on her. She'd have to wash, but not now. She had more important things to do! She had to solve the case!

Chapter 4

Millie was quiet as a mouse as she tiptoed through the dimly lit hallway and down the stairs. She stopped on the bottom landing. Everything was pitch black. Even though she was getting older and would be a pre-teen in a couple of years, she was still a little bit afraid of the dark.

The house was silent and scary. All the adults had gone to bed.

Startled by the sound of creaking floorboards, Millie quickly turned around. A parade of shadows was following her. It was the boys. Millie sighed with relief. She was glad it wasn't her parents, or grandparents, or one of her aunts or uncles. They wouldn't appreciate her prowling around the house so late at night.

"Be quiet," she snarled. "You're supposed to tiptoe down the stairs. You guys sound like a herd of elephants!"

The further down the stairs she went the darker it got. Millie held tight to the railing until she felt it end. She cautiously took the last step and extended her foot to make sure she was on the floor. There were sounds in the darkness: creepy, scary sounds. The wind was blowing. It rattled the windows and caused the weathervane on the shed to squeak and squeal as it changed direction with each gust. The house creaked and groaned. Its wooden beams bending and straining in the cold. Eerie knocking and scraping could be heard on the porch as the wind lifted the big wreath and repeatedly banged it into the front door. Clicks and whooshes were coming from under the floorboards. The radiators began to rumble and clank. Millie gulped. This reminded her of a scene from a horror movie. She felt a shiver go up her spine. She half expected a ghost, vampire, zombie, or crazy killer to jump out at her any minute. Millie hesitated a moment; then, finding her courage, walked off into the darkness.

If she was going to solve the mystery of why there weren't any presents under the Christmas tree this year, she'd have to look for clues. She needed to start the investigation in the last place Santa had been...the living room. Earlier in the evening, they'd left a Christmas Eve snack of milk and cookies for him there.

Millie walked fast, worried there might be scary things hiding in the shadows. Unable to see anything, she walked right into a half-closed door, banging her chin.

The boys followed her, setting off a chain reaction. One boy bumped into Millie. Then somebody bumped into him. And suddenly everybody was bumping into everybody else.

"Watch it!" she growled, rubbing her chin to ease the pain. "Everybody back up so I can get the door open."

They did as they were told, but in their rush began knocking into each other. Some of the boys lost their balance and fell against the wall.

She shook her head. How was she ever going to solve this case with these clowns trailing her?

"Stay out of my way!" she warned. "Don't walk! Don't talk! Don't try to help me! I don't want you messing things up! Do you understand?"

"Yes. Yup. Yeah. OK. Uh-huh," they whispered.

"Good," she snapped. "Now maybe I can get to work!"

Chapter 5

Millie walked through the door into the living room. It wasn't nearly as dark in there as it was in the rest of the house. The glow from the streetlight lit the room. She looked around. As her eyes became used to the light, she was able to make out the shadowy outlines of the couch and chairs, and the Christmas tree in the corner. She could also see the row of empty stockings hung above the fireplace.

Millie went to the picture window. On the table beside it she found an empty glass and a crumb-covered plate. She didn't know what to make of them.

Needing more light to conduct her investigation, she hurried back to the door.

"Well come in if you're coming!" she said to the boys who were waiting just outside.

They obediently filed into the room and watched as she shut the door behind them. Though she tried to do it as quietly as possible, the hinges let out a long, loud creak. Her eyes grew wide in alarm. She hoped none of the adults had heard it.

For a minute everyone stood perfectly still. Some with their eyes fixed on the ceiling. Others staring down at the floor. They were waiting to see if the noise had awakened the grown-ups. They were listening for the sound of footsteps coming up or going down the stairs. Thankfully there weren't any. Their parents and relatives were all sound sleepers.

Millie went from window to window peering out at the snow. There were footprints all over the place. They appeared to be under every window. As though Santa had been looking in. Why so many footprints? Had Santa brought a bunch of his elves along? Elves with very big feet? But why were the footprints on the ground? Shouldn't they be on the roof?

There was a pickup truck parked at the end of their driveway. She didn't recognize it. She was sure it didn't belong to anyone in her family. Or the neighbors either. It looked like the back of the truck was filled with bags. Bags of toys maybe? Since when did Santa start using a truck instead of a sleigh to deliver presents? He was driving instead of flying now? Not likely! Santa's sleigh was magic. That's why he could carry enough presents for all the boys and girls of the world in a single trip. Every time he pulled a toy out of his bag, a new one replaced it. Whoever heard of a magic pickup truck? That rusted out, dented, old clunker didn't look like it could make it to the other side of town, let alone around the world. She squinted. Those looked like garbage bags piled in the back of the truck, not a big sack brimming with toys. This was all very strange. Not like Santa at all!

She pulled down the shades and closed the drapes. Satisfied that no one could see in, Millie turned on the table lamp and set to work.

The boys watched as she brought the magnifying glass to her eye and began a careful examination of the evidence.

"Do you suppose she's looking for prints?" Peter asked.

Millie studied the glass. Then the plate. And finally the table. After a minute she picked something up off the table. It appeared to be a wad of soft, snow-white hair.

"Looks like Santa's losing his hair. Do you think he's going bald?" Vince asked his cousin Brian, who was standing just behind him.

"Maybe he's shedding," Brian replied, sounding uncertain. He looked at the other boys. They shrugged their shoulders.

"Our dog sheds," Vincent chimed in.

Millie picked up the glass and took a closer look. There were several hairs clinging to the rim. She held the glass up to the light. There was something stuck to the inside of the glass too. She stuck her fingers in and pulled out a few milk soaked hairs. She couldn't imagine how they'd gotten inside the glass. Could the hairs be from Santa's beard? She didn't think so. The hair was soft, not coarse.

"Hmmm..." she said as she walked away. She turned her attention to the fireplace and empty Christmas stockings.

The black metal fire screen had fallen or been pushed over. It was lying on the hearth. She dropped to her knees and peered into the firebox. The stack of kindling and logs her father had arranged for tomorrow morning's fire had not been disturbed. Neither had the pile of cinders and ashes around the grate. More importantly, there weren't any footprints in the ashes.

Millie set the screen to the side and ran her finger slowly across the gray marble hearth. To her surprise there was not one speck of ash or dust. How had Santa managed to come down the chimney and then leave the same way without leaving a trace? If Santa had already been here tonight, he must have come through a door or window, because he certainly hadn't gotten in this way!

She was replacing the screen when she noticed a red glass ball wedged behind the fireplace tools. It was one of her mother's favorite Christmas ornaments. It once belonged to her great grandmother. She'd brought it to America from her native Italy. What was it doing there? The tree was all the way across the room. Too far away for the ornament to have rolled over here. If someone had accidentally kicked it, the fragile ornament would have shattered into a hundred pieces. So then how did it get there?

Millie stood up. She was looking at the stockings. They were hanging limply from the wooden mantle. Her eyes suddenly widened. She reached out and grabbed the toe of each one. She looked both surprised and puzzled.

"What's wrong?" Chris Konitski asked Roger. He figured since he was her brother he might know what the look meant.

"I don't know!" said Roger. "Maybe it's a clue or something."

All the boys nodded in agreement. That was it all right…she'd found some sort of clue!

Chris was feeling brave. He spoke up. "Did you find something Millie?"

She lifted her hand to her head and scratched a time or two. She didn't bother answering his question.

"It must be something real important," Vincent whispered, trying not to disturb her concentration.

She spun around and faced them. "Something very strange is going on here!" Millie announced.

They looked at one another, nodding their heads. They'd suspected as much.

"Nothing about this makes any sense," Millie began. "I can't speak for you guys, but I know that I've been **very, very good** this year."

The boys looked guilty. Maybe they hadn't been quite as good as they should have been. They listened as she continued.

"If you're good, you get presents. Right?"

The boys nodded.

"And if you're bad, Santa stuffs your stocking with a big lump of coal. True?"

Again they nodded.

"Well in that case we're missing something," she informed them.

The boys looked around the room. What was it they were supposed to see? What was missing?

"Are you all blind? It's so obvious!" she told them.

It might have been obvious to her, but from the bewildered looks on their faces it certainly wasn't obvious to them.

Millie sighed and rolled her eyes. "Santa always leaves one or the other, *so...*" They stared at her blankly. "Oh for goodness sake, ***this isn't rocket science!***" she said giving them the answer. ***"Where's the coal?"***

The Konitski boys looked at each other. They shrugged their shoulders. The Rossis and the Larabees looked more confused than ever.

"I don't understand. Does that mean we've been good or bad?" Roger asked.

"It means that maybe things aren't what they appear to be," Millie told him. She dropped to her knees again to check the rug.

"What's she doing now?" Vincent asked, thinking his older brothers might know.

But both Peter and David were baffled. They didn't have the faintest idea what she was up to.

Using her magnifying glass, Millie examined every speck on the carpet.

"These are definitely cookie crumbs," she told the boys. Millie stared at the bits of cookie scattered around the room. She didn't remember Santa being such a messy eater before.

Suddenly Millie jumped to her feet and turned her attention back to the table. The boys were all eyes as she picked up the neatly folded paper napkin. Just as she'd suspected, it hadn't been used.

Had Santa forgotten his manners? Millie didn't think so. Santa was a gentleman and polite people always used a napkin.

She pushed back her bangs and began to scratch her head. She was thinking very hard.

"Do you suppose she's onto something?" Tom asked Roger.

"Yes," the little boy replied. His blue eyes followed his sister's every move.

She returned to the empty glass of milk. Millie studied the silky white hairs on the rim. They were baby fine. All appeared to be the same length, about two inches long. Then she turned her attention to the unusual smudges inside the glass. It looked as if someone had tried to lick the inside clean. Santa had better manners than that…didn't he?

"Do you think she's looking for fingerprints?" Brian asked.

"Could be," one of the Rossi boys whispered back. "It looks like she found something. Another clue maybe."

"She's a good detective," Brian said in admiration. "Just like the ones on TV."

Millie Muldoon looked at the glass, the plate, and the napkin. Then she turned to stare at the fireplace, the empty stockings, and the shiny Christmas ornament peeking out from behind the black metal tools. She tossed back her braids and smiled.

"That's a good sign isn't it?" Chris asked Roger.

Roger nodded. "Yup, I think it is," he said hopefully.

Chapter 6

Millie was crawling around the floor on her hands and knees. She stopped every once in a while to pick up a stray hair and examine it under her magnifying glass. Or to take a closer look at a cookie crumb she'd found. Millie circled the couch on all fours. Then scrambled over the chair. Across the footstool. And past the fireplace. She snaked between floor lamps, tables, and rockers. Finally making her way into the darkened dining room.

"I'll get the light," Vincent volunteered, hurrying to the switch.

Everybody gasped when the lights went on.

"Oh my goodness! Look at this place!" Chris said, shocked.

There were cookie crumbs everywhere. They were scattered all over the brown carpet. From one end of the room to the other.

"Santa really made a mess, didn't he?" Tom declared.

Everyone nodded. Surprised that Santa, of all people, should be so untidy.

"Your Mom is going to be real mad about this," David announced. His Aunt Sue would have a fit when she saw what Santa did. She liked things neat and tidy!

"Mommy's not going to yell at Santa is she Millie?" Roger

asked. He was worried that the old man's feelings might be hurt. He was sure Santa hadn't meant to dirty the rug. It was probably an accident.

His sister didn't answer. She was thinking. Millie looked around the room. She was searching for something.

"Aha!" she yelled, spotting Fluffy. Fluffy was her Great Aunt Priscilla Palermo's white Angora cat.

The cat was lying on a pink satin pillow in the corner of the room. She was very furry and very fat, and wore a blue jeweled collar.

Fluffy was a pretty cat. But she had a nasty disposition. She didn't like children. Millie and her cousins had the bites and scratches to prove it!

The cat stopped purring as Millie came closer. She didn't like being disturbed. Especially when she was trying to sleep.

Fluffy hissed at Millie. Then took a swipe at the girl with her front paw. The cat's claws were out.

"Bad Kitty," Millie scolded.

The cat arched her back. She made a threatening sound. It was part growl, part howl, part snarl.

Millie inched closer. The cat was watching her every move.

She opened her mouth, revealing her sharp, pointy teeth.

Fluffy didn't trust little humans. One minute they'd be petting you nicely. And the very next they'd be pulling your tail. Or holding you up by your paws and trying to make you walk on your hind legs. Or dressing you up in doll clothes. Or worse still, trying to give you a bubble bath in the kitchen sink!

Millie slowly extended her hand. She began stroking the cat's soft white fur. She was trying to make friends with the animal. But Fluffy didn't want to be pals. She lifted her paw, ready to scratch. But decided to yawn instead. She was sleepy and feeling lazy. Much too tired to put up a fuss! So she allowed Millie to pet her.

"Nice Kitty," Millie said as she studied Fluffy. A moment later she was smiling with happiness and relief.

"Did you find something else," David asked.

"I sure did. Here's the culprit," she announced, pointing at Fluffy.

"What?" Vince stared at her in surprise. "I don't understand. You think the cat had something to do with making this mess?"

"And our not getting any presents?" David wanted to know.

"That's exactly what I mean," she said. "See the white stuff all over the pillow?"

They nodded that they did.

"It's Fluffy's fur," Millie informed them. "She's shedding. That's what was all over the living room."

The boys looked surprised and a bit bewildered at the news.

"And see this?" she said, motioning them closer. She pointed to the cat's wet whiskers and damp fur. "That's from the milk. She lapped it up. Sticking her head further and further into the glass to get every last drop. It's a wonder she didn't knock the glass over."

"Shame on you," Roger scolded. "You've been a very bad kitty. Drinking Santa's milk like that! No wonder he didn't leave us any presents this year. It's all your fault cat!"

Millie glared at her little brother for interrupting her.

"Oops! Sorry!" he said meekly.

"As I was saying," she continued, "That's why there were hairs both inside and outside the glass," she explained.

"Boy you're sure smart," Tom said, obviously impressed with her detective skills.

Everyone nodded their agreement.

"But what about the cookies?" Brian asked. "Who ate them?"

"Yeah," Peter asked, puzzled. "Who did that?"

Millie shook her head and looked annoyed. These boys wouldn't know a clue if it was right in front of them. Even if it jumped up and bit them on the nose!

"Shoo," she demanded, waving her hands and trying to get Fluffy off the pillow. But the cat wouldn't cooperate. Seeing that she wasn't going to budge, Millie gently shoved her off her resting place. Underneath her was a half-eaten cookie, which she must have been saving for later, and a mound of crumbs. "Does this answer your question?" she asked.

Peter nodded, but Brian still looked confused.

"I don't understand," Brian said. "I get the part about the milk and cookies. And all the hair and stuff. But who moved the fireplace screen? Didn't Santa do that when he came down the chimney?"

"The cat did it," she told him. "I found a Christmas ornament behind the fireplace tools. I think Fluffy knocked it off the tree. She was probably batting it around, playing with it, when it got stuck back there. She must have been trying to get it out when she bumped into the screen. That's how it got tipped over."

"That sounds reasonable" Brian said.

"Uh Oh," Richard interrupted, suddenly looking horrified. "If Fluffy is the one who ate Santa's snack. And there are no presents under the tree. And no coal in our stockings. Then….then….that must mean that Santa hasn't come yet!"

"Exactly!" Millie said, sounding like a know-it-all.

"Is he going to be mad at us for still being up?" Roger worried.

"What are we going to do?" Tom whined. He always did that when there was trouble. It annoyed her no end!

"I want you all to go stand by the living room door. And I want you to be quiet. Very, very, very quiet! Got that?" she said sternly. "I'll to try to get this mess cleaned up."

Tom hurried off toward the door. The other boys were right behind him.

They were hoping Millie could straighten everything out.

Chapter 7

Wait a minute! Millie stopped short. Her smile changed to a frown. She'd only solved one part of the mystery. She'd explained what happened to the milk and cookies and how the fireplace screen got knocked over. But she'd yet to figure out who made the footprints!

While the boys waited, Millie walked through the downstairs. She checked every window and door. They were all locked. As she suspected, there were footprints in front of each one. It looked as if someone had been casing the house. ***Did Santa case houses?*** She didn't think so!

There were three sets of footprints in front of the patio door in the kitchen. They all had thick tread. Like they'd been made by heavy boots. One of them ***might*** have been Santa's. He did wear boots. But the other two appeared to be the same size and certainly weren't made by any pint-sized elves! She could see a broken piece of plastic in the snow. Millie was certain it was part of the outside door handle. ***What was going on here? It looked like someone had broken it off trying to get in!***

Millie felt a chill go up her spine when she noticed that the ladder her father kept stored under the porch was now standing upright and leaning against the house. Well that explained the noise on the roof the kids had heard

She noticed something odd at her next door neighbor's house. A small beam of light was bouncing around the Swan's family room. She was pretty sure it was coming from a flashlight. If the Swans were looking for something in that room, **why wouldn't they just turn on the lights?** Could their power be off? Millie checked the streetlights. They were on. Then she spotted the blue glow coming from the Swan's basement window. They had a fancy, new heating system down there that hung on the wall. It had a digital screen on the front that flashed blue numbers every minute or so. Their power was definitely on!

Millie's attention returned to the bouncing light upstairs. She could see the Swan's Christmas tree and the pile of presents underneath it. One by one, the presents were pulled out from under the tree until there were none left. Then the light went out. Millie tried to make sense of what she was seeing. Could Santa have delivered the wrong presents to the Swans? Was that why he was taking them back? She looked up at her neighbor's roof. **No reindeer! No sleigh! Whoever was over at the Swan's house...she was pretty sure it wasn't Santa!**

A few minutes later Millie let out a gasp. There was a shadowy figure sneaking out the Swan's back door. He was dressed in a red suit like Santa. But he wasn't the real thing! This Santa was skinny. He kept adjusting a big pillow that was supposed to be his belly. His beard was fake too. It was crooked and scraggly. And dark hair peeked out from the white wig he was wearing under his hat. He was carrying a big, black, garbage bag. It looked like it was filled with…with… ***Oh no!*** He was stealing the neighbor's Christmas present! ***Things were finally starting to make sense!***

Hadn't she heard on the news that a group of thieves called the "Jingle Bell Bandits" had been operating in their area? Stealing Christmas packages off people's porches? They'd been following delivery trucks around neighborhoods. As soon as the packages were delivered, if no one was home, they were stolen. They'd also broken into several homes and taken presents, jewelry, and other valuables. Most of the time they hit the houses while the owners were gone. But last week they changed their MO. They tied up and robbed two elderly couples and a lady who'd been home when they broke in. ***Could this be the same gang?***

Millie needed to do something! ***Now! Before they got away!***

She hurried to the counter and found her Mom's cellphone in its charger. Millie grabbed it and dialed 911. After explaining the situation to the dispatcher the woman said she'd send the police right over.

Millie went back into the living room. Peeking out the window, she watched as the thieves began piling their loot in the back of the truck. It looked like they'd hit most of the houses in the neighborhood. Except maybe this one! They hadn't gotten into her house...*at least not yet!* But it sure looked like they tried.

Millie strained to read the license plate, just in case the police didn't get here in time. But the plate was so dirty and banged up; she couldn't make it out. She didn't know the make and model of the truck either. She studied the pickup so she could describe it if she had to. It was mostly dark blue with a gray fender in front. There were dents in the door and back fender and it had a rusted front bumper.

She hoped the cops would hurry. **She didn't want everyone's Christmas ruined!**

Chapter 8

The boys watched as Millie hurried to clean up the mess that Fluffy made. She used the carpet sweeper to get all the crumbs off the rug. Then wiped the table and set out fresh milk and cookies for Santa Claus.

She seemed nervous. Every two minutes she'd peek out the window to see what was going on outside.

The sound of engines, skidding tires, and squeaking brakes drew everyone's attention to the front picture window. They all peered out. Four police cars had surrounded the truck. The officers quickly rounded up the gang of crooks and arrested them.

"What's going on?" her cousin David asked in alarm. "It looks like…" he stared out the window in disbelief. "**Oh no!** They just put handcuffs on Santa. It looks like they're arresting him."

Everyone let out a gasp. "They're arresting Santa? Why would they do that?" Vincent demanded to know." Are they crazy?"

"That's not Santa!" Millie informed him.

"Are you sure?" Roger pressed her. He looked like he was about to burst into tears.

"Yes I'm sure!"

"But…" Roger started to say something and then stopped. His eyes widened as he stared at the scene outside. "Holy cow!

There are four Santas outside. One. Two. Three. Four." He said, counting them. "And I think there's another one sitting in the truck. Are you sure one of them isn't the real Santa?"

"Positive! They're a gang of thieves. They've been breaking into houses and stealing people's presents," Millie explained.

"What? Wait!" Christopher was confused. "Santa was stealing presents? Why would Santa do that? He has warehouses full of them at the North Pole!"

Millie shook her head. Little boys could be dense sometimes. Especially this one. "I told you that's not Santa. ***None of them are Santa!*** They're crooks. I think they're a gang called the "Jingle Bell Bandits."

"How do you know that?" Christopher challenged.

"Because I saw one of them taking presents from our neighbor's house!"

"Oh," he responded meekly.

"But who called the police," Brian wanted to know.

"Who do you think?" Millie snapped, making a ***"duh"*** face.

"You?" Brian looked impressed.

Millie nodded.

"But how did you get onto the bandits in the first place?" her cousin Richard Konitski asked. "It was the cat that ate the cookies and drank the milk. She's the one who knocked over the fireplace screen."

"That's right! But the cat didn't make the noise on the roof, leave the footprints in the snow, or jiggle the door knob did she?"

They all shook their heads. No, she didn't!

"I had to figure out who did what! Fluffy also didn't put the ladder up against the side of the house or break the patio door handle trying to get in."

Their eyes widened in a mixture of fear and surprise at that bit of news.

"The bandits tried to break into this house?' Richard gulped.

"It certainly looks like they did," she replied. "The minute I saw all the footprints in the snow I knew there were two mysteries. Not just one. I followed the clues and was able to solve both of them."

"Did they get in? Did they steal our presents?" Richard asked horrified.

"No," Millie told him.

"How can you be so sure?"

"Because there's no evidence they ever got *into* the house. All the doors and windows are still locked. And there are no wet spots anywhere. And no footprints inside. It's windy outside. If they'd managed to pry open a window or force open a door, the snow would have blown in. Once it melted, it would have left a wet spot. The bandits were wearing boots. If they had gotten in they would have tracked snow through the house. There are no footprints! Not in the kitchen. Not at the front door. Not in the living room. ***They never made it into the house!***

"So then Santa *hasn't* come yet?" Vincent asked hopefully.

All eyes turned to Millie.

"No," she assured him.

Everyone looked relieved except for Vincent. He wasn't convinced. "So we still might get our presents?" he asked. He didn't want to be a pest. He just wanted to be sure he heard her right.

Before she could respond, Roger spoke up. "Will Santa still come tonight Millie?" he asked, worried. "If Santa flies over and sees that the police and the bad guys are still up. That they aren't in bed and fast asleep. Will he skip our house?" He was on the verge of tears.

"The police are allowed to stay up late on Christmas Eve!" she informed him. "They're working!"

"Oh!" Roger said. "But what about Santa?"

"I'm sure Santa Claus will come tonight. But he won't leave us any presents if he finds you guys standing around asking me a bunch of dumb questions!"

They looked at each other. Millie was right. Whatever questions they had could wait until morning…***after Santa had left their presents!***

When she was satisfied that everything looked neat and tidy again, Millie turned off the lights. She circled the room. Opening the drapes and raising the shades. When she was finished, she led the boys through the darkened house and back to bed.

Chapter 9

Everyone hurried into her room except for Roger. He stood in the doorway. He was giving her his sad cow look.

"I suppose you want to sleep in here too?" she grumbled. There were already seven boys too many in her room!

"Can I?" he asked. He hoped that just this once she'd be nice and say yes.

Millie sighed. It was Christmas after all. "I suppose so," she said, "But only this one time. Don't think this means you can come walking in here anytime you please! Understand?"

He nodded that he did.

"And don't ever tell any of my friends about this. Got that?"

Again he nodded. This time he was smiling.

"OK then, go get your sleeping bag. Park yourself over in the corner by the closet where you won't bother me too much."

He was off in a flash. After a minute he returned. He was dragging his super hero sleeping bag behind him.

Without saying a word, Millie pointed to where she wanted him. It was between Tom and Vincent. They liked to giggle, talk, and fool around. Maybe this would keep them quiet.

Careful not to step on anybody, Roger went right where

she'd told him. After spreading out his slumber bag, he crawled in. Roger turned and smiled at his big sister.

Millie rolled her eyes. Having the little pain around wasn't all that bad, she supposed. But all things considered…she'd still prefer having a poodle puppy rather than a little brother.

"Be quiet and go to sleep. All of you!" she ordered as she crawled into bed.

She searched under the sheet until she found Clarence her Teddy Bear. She gave him a big hug. Millie snuggled under the blanket and turned out the light.

"Millie?" a voice whispered to her from the darkness.

"What now," she grumbled.

"You're a real good detective!"

"Yeah, I know!" she snorted. "Now be quiet and go to sleep so Santa can come!"

The room grew quiet. The squirming and whispering stopped.

Millie closed her eyes and imagined riding down Maple Street hill on her shiny new, purple bike. She'd just drifted off to sleep when she heard bells jingling outside. ***Santa was here!*** She smiled. ***This was going to be the best Christmas ever!***

The End

A Note From Mary Vigliante Szydlowski

I hope you enjoyed reading Millie Muldoon & the Christmas Mystery.

If you did, I'd appreciate you leaving a positive review on the site where you

purchased the book.

Thank you!

Happy Reading!

About the Author

Mary Vigliante Szydlowski writes across several genres under several pseudonyms. Her published Science Fiction/Fantasy works include novels: **Dark Realm**, **The Ark** (Jarl Szydlow), **The Colony** (Mary Vigliante), **The Land** (Mary Vigliante), **Source of Evil** (Mary Vigliante), and a novella, **The Hand of My Enemy**.

She's the author of **Worship the Night**, a supernatural, psychological thriller, and a novel **Silent Song**. Under the pen name Mia Frances, she's also the author of the adult, romantic suspense, murder mystery series: **IN HIS KEEPING: TAKEN, BANISHED, and CLAIMED.**

Her other children's books are: Millie Muldoon & the Case of the Thanksgiving Turkey-napper, A Puddle for Poo, Kia's Manatee, The Duck in the Hole, and I Can't Talk, I've Got Farbles In My Mouth.

Her short stories, articles, children's stories, essays, and poems have appeared in anthologies, books, magazines, newspapers, and on the web.

Visit her website at:
http://www.maryviglianteszydlowski.com/

Made in United States
Troutdale, OR
12/21/2023

16265449R00031